Happy 1st Birthday
Christian!

Love Uncle Tom, Aunt Rene
& Bailey

Just Like Daddy

FRANK ASCH

Simon and Schuster Books for Young Readers
Published by Simon & Schuster Inc., New York

Published by Simon and Schuster Books for Young Readers
A Division of Simon & Schuster Inc.
Simon & Schuster Building
Rockefeller Center
1230 Avenue of the Americas
New York, NY 10020

10 9 8 7

10 9 8 7   pbk

Simon and Schuster Books for Young Readers
is a trademark of Simon & Schuster Inc.
Manufactured in the United States of America

Library of Congress Cataloging-in-Publication Data
Asch, Frank.   Just like daddy.
Summary: A very young bear describes all the activities
he does during the day that are just like his daddy's.
[1. Fathers and sons—Fiction.   2. Bears—Fiction]
I. Title.   PZ7.A778Ju
1988   [E]   88-6570
ISBN 0-671-66456-5
ISBN 0-671-66457-3 (pbk.)

To Devin

When I got up this morning
I yawned a big yawn…

Just like Daddy.

I washed my face, got dressed,
and had a big breakfast...

Just like Daddy.

Then I put on my coat
and my boots…

Just like Daddy.

And we all went fishing.

On the way I picked a flower
and gave it to my mother…

Just like Daddy.

When we got to the lake,
I put a big worm on my hook...

Just like Daddy.

All day we fished and fished,
and I caught a big fish…

Just like Mommy!

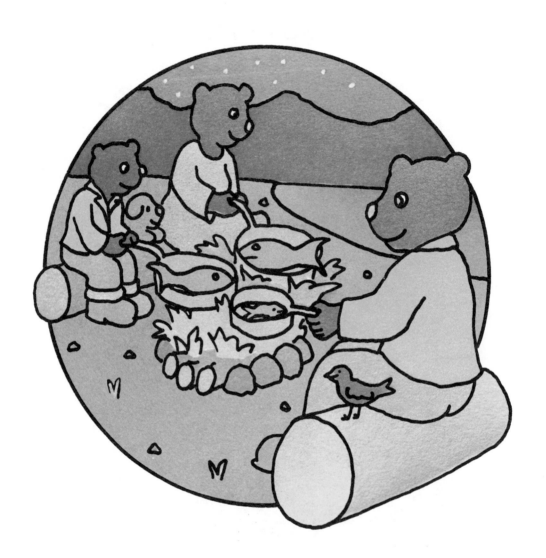